The
Robert Munsch
Paper Bag
Michael Martchenko
Princess

The Story Behind the Story

Developed by the editors at Annick Press with Sarah Dann

annick press
Toronto • New York • Vancouver

Every effort has been made to trace copyright holders and gain permission for use of the images in this book. If there are any inadvertent omissions, we apologize to those concerned and ask that they contact the publisher.

We acknowledge the support of the Canada Council for the Arts, the Ontario Arts Council, and the Government of Canada through the Canada Book Fund (CBF) for our publishing activities.

Cataloging in Publication

Munsch, Robert N., 1945-
    The paper bag princess 25th anniversary edition : the story behind the story / Robert Munsch, Michael Martchenko ; developed by the editors at Annick Press with Sarah Dann.

Includes bibliographical references.
ISBN 1-55037-915-1

    I. Martchenko, Michael II. Dann, Sarah, 1970- III. Title.

PS8576.U575P36 2005   jC813'.54   C2005-902859-9

The text was typeset in Adobe Jenson.

Distributed in Canada by:
Firefly Books Ltd.
50 Staples Avenue, Unit 1
Richmond Hill, ON
L4B 0A7

Published in the U.S.A. by Annick Press (U.S.) Ltd.
Distributed in the U.S.A. by:
Firefly Books (U.S.) Inc.
P.O. Box 1338
Ellicott Station
Buffalo, NY 14205

Printed in China.

Visit us at: www.annickpress.com

Acknowledgments

The publisher wishes to thank Tara Blue, Joel Kaiser, Cherry Karpyshin, Norbert Kondracki, Marcy Meyer, Jill Pring, Mountain Park Elementary School, Chase, Jonas, Cody, Kaylie, Parker, Tyler, Jessica, Matthew, Aubrey, and Elizabeth.

To Elizabeth.
—R.M.

To Robert Munsch, Anne Millyard,
and Rick Wilks for giving me the
opportunity of a lifetime.
—M.M.

Contents

Happy Birthday, ★ Paper Bag Princess

Have you wondered how publishing companies decide which stories they are going to publish? At Annick Press we believe in books that make you think about things in new ways. And what can be more fun than a story that is so good you want to hear it again and again? These are the qualities we loved so much in *The Paper Bag Princess* from the very first time we read it.

We vividly remember the day the story arrived in the mail. We had read many princess stories, but never one that featured a spunky, quick-witted girl like Elizabeth. Following a short discussion, we had only one question: what was Robert Munsch's telephone number? We had to tell him that Annick would publish his manuscript right away!

As much as we wished we could announce the publication of *The Paper Bag Princess* that very week, it doesn't work that way. In fact, it takes a year or so to create a book. There are all kinds of decisions and choices that have to be made, including polishing the story so that it reads as well as it possibly can and finding an illustrator to draw the pictures. Here's the story of how that manuscript received in the mail became a book, and how that book went on to become a beloved and treasured story for millions of people.

Happy Birthday, Paper Bag Princess!

Rick Wilks and Anne W. Millyard

Annick Press founders Anne Millyard and Rick Wilks, circa 1980.

6

Robert Munsch

THE STORY OF A STORYTELLER

One of the world's best-known children's authors sure didn't start out as much of a writer. Robert Norman Munsch was born into a family of nine kids in Pittsburgh, Pennsylvania. He didn't do so well all through school, and he insists he never learned to spell properly. Even so, he always liked to write poetry, and silly poems were his particular favorite.

A young Robert Munsch bundled up in inspiration for a future story.

By the time he was a teenager, things didn't seem as funny. He didn't get along with anybody in high school, and he spent most of his time reading books. One book he was particularly interested in was the Bible. So, after graduating, he decided to study to become a Catholic priest.

Bob performs in his early days as an author. Despite his international success, he never expected to be a writer.

7

For seven years he studied to be a priest, only to learn that it wasn't for him. But during that time he helped out at an orphanage where he discovered that he loved working with kids. And so, after leaving his studies behind, Bob Munsch started working at a daycare.

He quickly learned that telling stories before naptime was a great trick for settling the kids down. Over the next ten years, he told hundreds of stories that he made up himself. Along the way he earned a degree in child studies, met his wife, and moved to Guelph, Ontario, in Canada.

One day, at the University of Guelph preschool lab where Bob now worked, his boss heard the stories and made him write them down and send them to book publishers.

Nine publishers said "no." One publisher said "yes." The books *Mud Puddle* and *The Dark* were published by Annick Press in 1979. Robert Munsch had become a writer of books for children.

Michael Martchenko

A PORTRAIT OF THE ARTIST

Around the time that Bob Munsch was writing down his stories for the first time, artist Michael Martchenko was working for an advertising agency. Unlike Bob, Michael always knew what he wanted to do for a living: draw pictures.

Michael grew up in a small town north of Paris, France. There weren't a lot of comic books there, but little Michael loved the ones he could find. In fact, he eventually learned to draw by copying the artwork he saw in comics starring the likes of Bugs Bunny and Daffy Duck. It wasn't long before he was drawing new adventures for his favorite characters.

When Michael was seven years old, he moved with his mother and sister to Canada. During the ocean crossing, Michael remembers ordering dinner one night on the ship and wanting peas with his meal. "I couldn't speak English," he recalls. "So I drew a pea pod for the waiter. That was my first commercial job. Art for food."

Once in Canada, Michael's family moved a lot so his mother could find work. Wherever he went, Michael gained a reputation at school as an artist. He was asked over and over again to decorate posters for plays and concerts. By high school, he even had his own comic strip ("which was pretty bad," he laughs) in the school paper.

After high school, Michael completed art college and began looking for a job as an illustrator. It wasn't easy at first – nobody was hiring artists – but eventually he found work at an advertising agency drawing storyboards for television commercials. From there, Michael would go on to a successful career as an art director and designer for other ad agencies and art studios. Michael was now earning more than peas for his art, but not for illustrating children's books. Not yet.

The Beginning of a Beautiful Partnership

It was while working at the ad agency that Michael first met Robert Munsch. Bob and the Annick Press publishers were on the hunt for an artist. They had a story called *The Paper Bag Princess*, and they needed an illustrator who could bring the spunky characters to life.

One night in 1979, Bob and his publishers went to a party at Michael's ad company. The party was a sort of show-and-tell of work by the company's artists. "We got there and took a quick look around," remembers Bob, "but all we saw were ads. We turned around to go because that wasn't what we needed. Then on the way out we saw a funny painting."

Michael had helped to hang all the advertising samples for the party. There was one spot that needed to be filled, but they had run out of ads. Michael had decided to bring in one of his fun works from home. The painting showed a flock of seagulls with wheels for feet coming in for a landing like airplanes. It was more than a little silly … and exactly what Bob and Annick were looking for.

Birds of a feather: this painting by Michael Martchenko caught the eye of Robert Munsch and Annick Press.

"They wanted to know if I'd like to draw pictures for a children's book," recalls Michael. "I thought, why not? That could be fun." And so Michael and Robert teamed up for what would be the first – and the most famous – of the more than 30 children's books they would create together. *The Paper Bag Princess*, still only words on a page, was about to get a face.

Would the Real Elizabeth Please Stand Up?

Elizabeth at age four, around the time she, and her coat, dropped by Bob's daycare.

Like his other stories, *The Paper Bag Princess* began as a naptime invention at a daycare where Bob worked. One day at the Bay Area Childcare Center in Coos Bay, Oregon, Bob had just finished telling yet another story about a prince rescuing a princess from a dragon. Bob's wife, who had been listening, asked, "Why can't the princess ever save the prince, Bob?" Bob thought this was a good question. He decided to create a new story about a princess who does the saving.

For Bob, part of the fun of storytelling is using the names of the kids that he meets. *The Paper Bag Princess* was no exception. As with all his stories, Bob told this one over and over again for years, changing it a little bit each time to make it better, and each time he would use the name of a girl who was listening.

Shortly before Bob turned the story into a book, he was working at the Family Studies Preschool at the University of Guelph in Ontario, Canada. It was there

that he met a young girl named Elizabeth Moziar. "When she came to the pre-school for the first time," Bob recalls, "she dropped her coat on the floor and waited for me to hang it up. I thought 'Wow! This kid thinks she is a princess.'" When Bob wrote down his princess story for Annick Press, he decided to keep Elizabeth's name.

The real Elizabeth didn't mind at all. She was seven years old when *The Paper Bag Princess* was published for the first time, in 1980. The book arrived in the mail with a letter from Bob. "I remember my mother putting the package on her ironing board and reading me the letter.

Dear Elizabeth

Here is a story that I used your name for. I hope you like it. I wanted to have Princess Elizabeth punch Ronald in the nose at the end but my publisher didn't let me do that. I hope you are fine. We have just adopted a baby named Andrew. I still teach in the preschool. How are you?

Bob

Elizabeth received this letter from Robert Munsch when she was seven years old.

13

Elizabeth

Elizabeth, all grown up, on her wedding day posing with her parents' dog, Fergie.

I was only seven and didn't fully understand what it meant, but I still remember that moment." Little did she suspect that the Paper Bag Elizabeth would go on to become a storybook princess almost as famous as Cinderella or Sleeping Beauty.

"It's amazing to me now," the grown-up Elizabeth says, "that the book is read by so many people. It's even studied in feminist literature classes! My own kids are still too young, but I look forward to reading all of Bob's books with them."

Today, Elizabeth is married and has a young son and a younger daughter. She teaches French in Guelph and still keeps in touch with Robert Munsch.

From Paper Bag to Paperback

HOW CHILDREN'S BOOKS ARE MADE

Making a picture book isn't as easy as it looks – especially not in 1980, when most publishers weren't yet using computers. Even with computers, there are many stages a storybook goes through before it gets to you. Here's how it usually works:

1. From Think to Ink: First, a writer turns an idea into a story and writes that story down on paper. Most authors will rewrite a story several times before letting anyone read it. Each time, they make changes to make the story better. Bob makes these changes through telling, not writing. In fact, he never writes down a story until he's told it many, many times to groups of kids. "I'm a storyteller first and a writer second," he says. "The stories change over time. Children respond to different parts, get bored in some parts, and I change them based on their response." Only then does he write the story on paper. This paper copy of the story is called a manuscript and has no pictures.

2. Let it Get Edited: When happy with the story, the author gives the manuscript to a publisher to read. A publisher is a person whose company decides which stories to make into books. The publisher and the author talk about how to make the story even better. The author rewrites the story again until it's just right. All this talking and rewriting is called editing.

3. Next Part's the Art: Once the story is at its best, the publisher finds an artist to make the pictures. This illustrator then makes simple black and white drawings called sketches. The illustrator talks with the publisher and the author about which sketches work well, and then the illustrator turns them into color paintings.

4. A Fine Design: When the words are done, and when the pictures are ready, they both need to be put together. The designer is the person who carefully arranges the words and pictures as they will look on the pages of the book and on the front and back covers. This work used to be done by cutting and pasting the words and pictures onto big pasteboards, which were then photographed. Today, it is usually done using scanners and computers.

5. Pressed for Time: Almost done! All that's left is to turn those photos or computer files into real books. This is done by a printing company, which uses a large machine, called a printing press, that presses coloured ink onto wide sheets of paper. Other machines then cut and fold and bind the paper into a book with a cover. A modern printing press can print as many as 176,000 color pages in an hour – that's almost 50 pages per second!

6. Where the Wares Are: Once the books are printed, the printer puts them into boxes and sends them to the publisher's warehouse – a large building where all the books are stored. The publisher then ships boxes of books to bookstores and libraries all over the country.

7. A Storybook Ending: At the bookstore or library, the staff unpacks the books and puts them on a shelf, where they wait to be picked up and read by someone like you.

17

She Ought to Be in Pictures

ILLUSTRATING THE PAPER BAG PRINCESS

Michael Martchenko was practiced at telling stories with pictures. From the comics he'd drawn as a kid to the storyboards he was now drawing professionally, Michael had learned many tricks to showing story information in pictures. So, when he agreed to illustrate *The Paper Bag Princess*, he wasn't worried that he had never worked on a picture book before.

He was worried, though, that it would be just another princess story … until the publishers gave him the manuscript. "They said it was a story about a prince, a princess, and a dragon," remembers Michael. "I thought, 'gee, that's not very original.' But then I read it and I thought, 'hey, this is pretty cool!'" With his interest snared, it wasn't long before Michael was hard at work bringing the story to life.

A COPY OF THE MANUSCRIPT MICHAEL USED TO CREATE THE ILLUSTRATIONS

You can see where he divided the story by which page the words will appear on. Michael still uses this method to decide which words to turn into pictures. "I look at the manuscript and think, 'well, this can go together, and I see how this could work well in a picture.'" Michael's decisions are then discussed with the publisher. Once pictures are added, some words may need to change to better fit the image, while others may not be needed anymore and are taken out completely. But words aren't the only things that change during this process.

18

PAPER BAGS AND PRINCES
~~ELIZABETH~&~DRAGON~~

Copyright Robert N. Munsch

When Elizabeth was a very beautiful princess she lived in a castle and had expensive princess clothes. She was going to marry a prince named Ronald.

Unfortunately, a dragon smashed her castle, burned all her clothes with its fiery breath and carroed off Prince Ronald.

Elizabeth decided to chase the dragon and get Ronald back. She looked all over for something to wear and the only thing she could find that was not burnt was a paper bag. So she put on the paper bag and followed the dragon. The dragon was easy to follow because it left a trail of burnt forests and horse's teeth.

Finally, Elizabeth came to a cave with a large door that had a huge knocker on it. She took hold of the knocker and banged on the door. The dragon stuck its nose out of the door and said, "Go away. I havw already eaten two kindergartens and a hospital and I still have a prince to eat. Come back and I will eat you tomorrow." It slammed the door so fast that Elizabeth almost got her nose caught.

Elizabeth grabbed hold of the knocker and banged on the door again. The dragon stuck its nose out the door and said, "Go away. I have already eaten two kindergartens and a hospital and I still have a prince to eat. Come back and I will eat you tomorrow." "Wait," shouted Elizabeth. "Is it true that lyou are the smartest and fiercest dragon in the whole world?" "Yes!" said the dragon.

"Is it true," said Elibabeth, "that you can burn up ten forests with your fiery breath?" "Oh, yes," said the dragon and it took a huge, deep breath andssbreathed out so much fire that it burnt up fifty forests.

ORIGINAL
ILLUSTRATION
FOR ELIZABETH'S
BURNED CLOTHES

It was tricky to show Elizabeth after the dragon burns off her clothes without showing her naked. Michael's first try made Elizabeth look too much like a caveman. In the final picture, Michael used a well-placed cloud of dust to protect the princess's dignity.

20

EARLY SKETCH FOR THE SLEEPING DRAGON

Sometimes both the words and the pictures changed in the creative process. In an earlier version of Bob's manuscript, Elizabeth tries to wake the dragon by shouting and stomping on his head, as shown in this sketch. But the book was running out of pages that could have pictures. Michael decided to combine the sleeping dragon and Prince Ronald waving for help into the same picture.

ORIGINAL SKETCH FOR RONALD'S RESCUE

The ending of *The Paper Bag Princess* is now world famous: the snotty prince doesn't want to be rescued by Elizabeth because she's a mess. In the original story, Elizabeth bops him one for being so rude and ungrateful, as you can see in this sketch. But hitting people — even arrogant princes who just might deserve it — isn't appropriate, and Bob and his publishers decided to take it out. Instead, Elizabeth tells off the so-called prince and then leaves him behind, proving that true nobility has nothing to do with appearances and everything to do with behavior.

22

Also famous is the last picture in
The Paper Bag Princess, which shows
Elizabeth skipping off happily
toward the sunset. Michael's earlier
idea for that image was to have
Elizabeth tossing away her paper
bag dress, as shown here. The
picture was funny and showed her
new-found freedom . . . but it also
showed a lot more. In the picture
that was finally used, of Elizabeth
skipping, she is still wearing her
bag. That image went on to become
the logo for Annick Press.

23

And now here's the story ...

The Paper Bag Princess

Story • Robert Munsch   Art • Michael Martchenko

Elizabeth was a beautiful princess. She lived in a castle and had expensive princess clothes. She was going to marry a prince named Ronald.

Unfortunately, a dragon smashed her castle, burned all her clothes with his fiery breath, and carried off Prince Ronald.

Elizabeth decided to chase the dragon and get Ronald back.

She looked everywhere for something to wear, but the only thing she could find that was not burnt was a paper bag. So she put on the paper bag and followed the dragon.

He was easy to follow, because he left a trail of burnt forests and horses' bones.

Finally, Elizabeth came to a cave with a large door that had a huge knocker on it. She took hold of the knocker and banged on the door.

The dragon stuck his nose out of the door and said, "Well, a princess! I love to eat princesses, but I have already eaten a whole castle today. I am a very busy dragon. Come back tomorrow."

He slammed the door so fast that Elizabeth almost got her nose caught.

Elizabeth grabbed the knocker and banged on the door again.

The dragon stuck his nose out of the door and said, "Go away. I love to eat princesses, but I have already eaten a whole castle today. I am a very busy dragon. Come back tomorrow."

"Wait," shouted Elizabeth. "Is it true that you are the smartest and fiercest dragon in the whole world?"

"Yes," said the dragon.

"Is it true," said Elizabeth, "that you can burn up ten forests with your fiery breath?"

"Oh, yes," said the dragon, and he took a huge, deep breath and breathed out so much fire that he burnt up fifty forests.

"Fantastic," said Elizabeth, and the dragon took another huge breath and breathed out so much fire that he burnt up one hundred forests.

"Magnificent," said Elizabeth, and the dragon took another huge breath, but this time nothing came out. The dragon didn't even have enough fire left to cook a meatball.

Elizabeth said, "Dragon, is it true that you can fly around the world in just ten seconds?"

"Why, yes," said the dragon, and jumped up and flew all the way around the world in just ten seconds.

He was very tired when he got back, but Elizabeth shouted, "Fantastic, do it again!"

So the dragon jumped up and flew around the whole world in just twenty seconds.

When he got back he was too tired to talk, and he lay down and went straight to sleep.

Elizabeth whispered, very softly, "Hey, dragon." The dragon didn't move at all.

She lifted up the dragon's ear and put her head right inside. She shouted as loud as she could, "Hey, dragon!"

The dragon was so tired he didn't even move.

Elizabeth walked right over the dragon and opened the door to the cave.

There was Prince Ronald. He looked at her and said, "Elizabeth, you are a mess! You smell like ashes, your hair is all tangled and you are wearing a dirty old paper bag. Come back when you are dressed like a real princess."

"Ronald," said Elizabeth, "your clothes are really pretty and your hair is very neat. You look like a real prince, but you are a bum."

They didn't get married after all.

And they lived happily ever after

A SUCCESS STORY

In the fall of 1980, *The Paper Bag Princess* hit the bookstores. Canada's national newspaper, *The Globe and Mail*, immediately raved, "*The Paper Bag Princess* is witty, vibrant and original." Another reviewer cheered, "I love to see the princess finally playing the role of hero." But not all critics were as pleased. One magazine predicted the book would be short-lived, declaring it "a picture book full of clichés." Would readers feel the same way?

After three years the book had sold **5,000 copies.**

To date, the book has sold over **3,000,000 copies.**

After three years the book had sold 5,000 copies, officially becoming a best-seller, and sales showed no signs of slowing down. Children loved the story, and their parents, teachers, and librarians loved its message. One *New York Times* writer confessed, "I pass along paperback copies to my sisters and friends as if it were a subversive leaflet." As Bob sees it, the reason for the book's universal popularity is simple. "This story is a success because it is real," he says. "There are no princes but there are a lot of bums, and you don't want to marry one."

Twenty-five years later, Princess Elizabeth continues to inspire readers. To date, the book has reprinted 52 times, sold over three million copies, and been enjoyed by countless readers. The story has now crossed generations – those who loved the book as kids are reading it to their own children – and has even traveled around the world. Not bad for a girl dressed only in paper.

Those who loved the book as kids are reading it to their own children.

★ ★ ★ ★ ★ ★ ★ ★ **51**

Around the World in Just Ten Seconds

THE PRINCESS GOES GLOBAL

Swedish ★

Hebrew

Elizabeth – she warms my heart, she gives me hope, I'd almost given up! Then she appeared – feisty, fearless, believing in herself, trusting her own instincts and intelligence as if it were obvious ... as it ought to be!

And so I brought her to life on stage – she spoke in Hebrew, Arabic, and English.

—lindi g. papoff
THEATER DIRECTOR, HAIFA, ISRAEL

P.S. How is it that everything in the forest burns except for her paper bag?

종이 봉지 공주

Korean

For the readers of *The Paper Bag Princess*:
Be strong and never doubt yourself! We are all special in our own unique way.

—Avril Lavigne
GRAMMY-NOMINATED AND MULTI-PLATINUM SINGER AND SONGWRITER, NAPANEE, CANADA

52

Armenian

Okay, maybe it took longer than ten seconds (only dragons can go that quickly), but in the past 25 years *The Paper Bag Princess* has indeed traveled around the world. The story has been translated into more than a dozen languages and continues to inspire readers in countries across the globe.

Arabic

British

Japanese

Spanish

German

Elizabeth was not so much ahead of her time, but right on time. For all in search of a strong, clever role model, look no further than our fearless heroine. Our young princess's handling of pesky dragons and arrogant royalty inspired my students and me. Self-respect and confidence in one's self are her gifts to girls and boys alike. However, Ronalds are forewarned: this may not be the fable for you.

—Christopher Garcia
EARLY CHILDHOOD EDUCATOR, EL PASO, TEXAS

De prinses in de papieren zak

Dutch

Prinses Papierzak

Flemish

Chinese

Welsh

As a social worker in family services I was working with young couples then expecting their first child. The values expressed in this book met with their full approval! This princess matched the advent of equal rights, where self-respect and the courage to stand up for one's convictions were more important than appearance.

—Hilde Becker
SOCIAL WORKER
BERLIN, GERMANY

★ 53

From the Best-Selling Book ...

THE PAPER BAG SPINOFFS

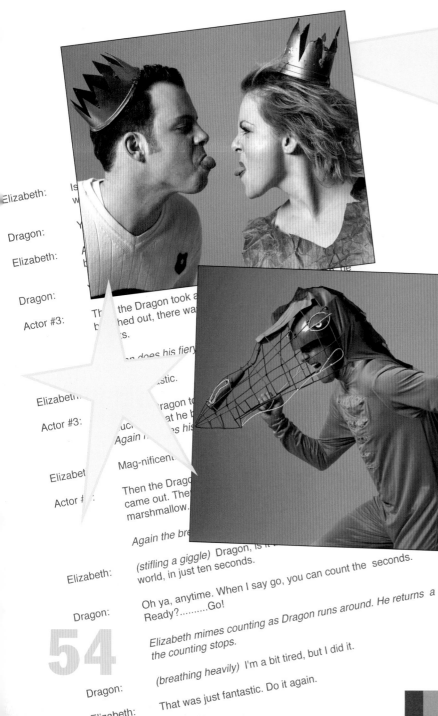

After the book's success, other kinds of artists wanted to explore different ideas for telling such a great story. Bob had already changed *The Paper Bag Princess* from a tell-out-loud story to a book with pictures, so why not let others have a try? And so, Annick and Bob gave special permission to certain companies to retell the story in fun and interesting ways. Soon Princess Elizabeth's adventures were being performed by real live actors, by puppets, and even by cartoons.

Above: Images from The Blue Collar Dance Company production of *The Paper Bag Princess* – a musical. Behind: A page from the script for *Munsch Alley*.

Above and right: Various performances of *The Paper Bag Princess* by Touring Players Theatre. Joel Kaiser, writer and director of *Munsch Alley*, remembers the New York cast's first show: "When the actress playing Elizabeth jumped out from behind the set in her underwear, the surprised and excited reaction from a theater full of kids almost blew her off the stage."

Below: A no-strings-attached performance of *Puppet Munsch* by the Prairie Theatre Exchange.

55

MORE PAPER BAG PRINCESS SPINOFFS

With all the versions of the story out there, there has certainly been plenty of princess to go around. Though the book form of *The Paper Bag Princess* remains the most popular, it is fun to see all the places where Elizabeth has popped up.

★ "Annikin" (mini-book) editions of the book.

★ Audio cassettes of the story told by Bob himself.

★ A cartoon version of the story available on video and DVD.

★ This storytelling kit based on the book includes plush characters and scenery.

★ Princess Elizabeth doll complete with paper bag dress.

Ever read a book using only your fingers? Visually impaired readers do it all the time. A special alphabet called Braille uses patterns of raised dots instead of printed letters to spell out the words of the story. But what about the pictures? That's where tactile books come in. These special books use textured, three-dimensional versions of the pictures that let visually impaired readers feel the shape of each scene. (This is the only time you should ever touch a dragon.)

A Braille edition of *The Paper Bag Princess*. The raised dots are on a clear plastic sheet that lies overtop of the printed page. That way, sighted readers can share the story too.

A tactile edition of *The Paper Bag Princess*. The shapes and textures are designed to match the original illustrations. Tactile books also include the story in Braille.

Thinking Outside the Bag

SURPRISE APPEARANCES BY LIZZIE

The Paper Bag Princess - holding out for Mr Right.

Later in life she met her true soul-mate
Prince Robert - who asked her to marry him.

In 2005, Michael Martchenko was contacted by a young man named Robert who was planning to propose to his girlfriend, Miriam. Because she was such a big fan of *The Paper Bag Princess*, Michael agreed to create this picture. Robert displayed the final colour painting in an art gallery and then led Miriam to it. She said yes (and did not call him a bum).

Every winter, Michael likes to create his own Christmas cards to send to family, friends, and people he has worked with. He illustrated this festive scene for the holiday season in 2001.

♫ Chestnuts Roasting Over An Open Fire ♫

This tattoo is on the belly of Janet T. Planet, a successful graphic and fashion designer, mechanical engineer, and creative director living in Los Angeles. "I felt inspired with the idea that she would remind me to watch out for dragons and arrogant princes and that sometimes being independent and on your own is the best option! I have had the tattoo for 10 years now, and she still reminds me of this wisdom every day!"

In November 2000, the television series *Life and Times* aired a biography of Robert Munsch. The producers asked Michael Martchenko to create some silly portraits of Bob based on his books, including this one for *The Paper Bag Princess*.

A fixture in libraries across North America, *The Paper Bag Princess* receives special attention at this school. Students from Mountain Park Elementary in Roswell, Georgia, pose with a giant painting of the cover.

59

Dear Mr. Munsch

KIDS RESPOND TO *THE PAPER BAG PRINCESS*

I like the dragon. He had to waste his fire. He must be tired!

I like the Paper Bag Princess. The funniest part was at the end when the princess said, "You are a bum."

The dragon fired down the castle. Then took prince Ronald. And went away. But Elezabeth followed the dragon.

I like the part where the dragon burnes all his fire up. I was so funny.

Dear Robert Munsch,
you stories are amazing I love The Story The paperbag princess it is very funy my favorite part of the Paperbag Princess is when the dragon loses all his fire breath. I wold like if you make a story about a very very famous soccer plaer. Why did you choose this job?

sincerely,
Jessica.

Dear Robert Munsch
When did you start writing? My Favorite book is the Paper Bag Princess. You are one of my favorite authors. Have a nice day.

From, Aubrey

By Aubrey

61

It's certainly been an amazing quarter-century for The *Paper Bag Princess*. So how does it feel to be responsible for a story that has had an impact on so many people? "I'm very grateful," reflects Michael. "Thanks to that sooty, messy-haired, badly dressed little princess, I've been able to fulfill my longtime wish to be a full-time children's book illustrator."

As for Bob, he remains impressed by the story's staying power:

"A paper bag
Does not last long,
It burns or blows away.
But now that mine is 25,
I think it's here to stay."

Robert Munsch

Michael Martchenko

Happy 25th birthday, Paper Bag Princess! May you enjoy many more.

The End?

63

Credits

PAGE 6 Photo: Paul Orenstein
PAGE 7 Photo, top: Courtesy Robert Munsch. Photo, bottom: Chris Bell
PAGE 9 Photo: Courtesy Michael Martchenko
PAGE 12 Photo: Courtesy Elizabeth
PAGE 14 Photo: Trina Koster Photography
PAGE 24 Photo: Pete Paterson
PAGE 52 Arabic edition: Tamer Institute
PAGE 53 British edition: Scholastic Children's Books. Japanese edition: Kawai Shuppan. Spanish edition: Susaeta Ediciones. German edition: Lappan Verlag. Chinese edition: Wisdom Cultural Medium, Inc. Welsh edition: Houdmont
PAGE 54 Production of *The Paper Bag Princess – A Musical*. Written by Joe Slabe. Directed by Marilyn Potts. Conceived and choreographed by Tara Blue. Produced by The Blue Collar Dance Company. With Jamie Tognazzini as Princess Elizabeth, Patrick MacEachern as Prince Ronald, and Gerald Matthews as the Dragon. Photos courtesy The Blue Collar Dance Company. Photos by Trudie Lee Photography.
Script: Courtesy Touring Players Theatre of Canada
PAGE 55
Top left: The Paper Bag Princess and Other Stories (1988). Written by Irene Watts. Directed and designed by Joel Kaiser. Produced by Touring Players Theatre of Canada. With Margarita Miniovich as Princess Elizabeth and Greg Armstrong-Morris as Prince Ronald. Photo courtesy Touring Players Theatre of Canada.
Top right: The Magic of Munsch (1997, Can.) Written, directed and designed by Joel Kaiser. Produced by Touring Players Theatre of Canada. With Kristin Booth as Princess Elizabeth and Christopher Furlong as Prince Ronald. Photo courtesy Touring Players Theatre of Canada.
Right centre (princess in bag and princess in underwear):
Munsch Alley (1997, U.S.) Written, directed and designed by Joel Kaiser. Produced by Touring Players Theatre of Canada. With Shari Berman as Princess Elizabeth. Photo courtesy Touring Players Theatre of Canada.
Bottom: Puppet Munsch. Based on the stories of Robert Munsch. Adapted and directed by Mariam Bernstein. Set, puppet, props and costume design by Shawn Kettner. Puppet builders: Crispi Porat and Kristi Friday. Lighting design: Eric Bosse. Stage manager: Amanda Smart. Featuring Kristi Friday as the Princess, Jason Neufeld as the Dragon, and Crispi Porat. Produced by Prairie Theatre Exchange, Dec. 2002. Photo and program courtesy of Prairie Theatre Exchange. Photo by Bruce Monk. "Puppet Munsch" logo by Tétro Design Inc.
PAGE 56 Storytelling kit: Lakeshore Learning Materials.
Videotape: The Cookie Jar Company. Audio tapes: Moonjin Media Co. Ltd. Princess Elizabeth doll, Annikins: Annick Press.
PAGE 57 *Left:* A Living Picture Book adaptation for blind and partially sighted children produced by The Living Paintings Trust, U.K.
Right: Tactile illustrations by Marcy Meyer, courtesy Sacramento Braille Transcribers, Inc. Transcribed (2000) by Charles Campbell. Reformatted (2005) by Dorothy Johnson. Sacramento Braille Transcribers, Inc. Sacramento, California. In one volume. Braille pages p1-p2 and 1-12.
PAGE 59 Photo: Dave Kelley. Artwork: Debi Embry
PAGES 62, 63 and Back Cover: Photos: Pete Paterson

Other books in the Classic Munsch series written by Robert Munsch and illustrated by Michael Martchenko

Other Classic Munsch Books